I CAN READ ABOUT

WITCHES

Written by Robyn Supraner   Illustrated by Frank Brugos

Troll Associates

All was sad and gloomy in the small town of Pleasantville. The town and its people were under a dark and terrible spell.

Nobody laughed. Nobody giggled. Nobody even smiled. A wicked old witch had robbed them of their laughter and had left them sad and blue.

Every smile and giggle and grin and chuckle was locked away in the deep, dark cellar of the nasty, old witch.

Pleasantville wasn't pleasant anymore. Best friends fought and hit each other. Babies cried. Mothers and fathers scolded. Brothers and sisters scratched and bit and wouldn't share their toys.

Without the gift of laughter, everything looked grim and gray. Nobody could remember how good it felt to smile. Nobody, except one little girl.
Her name was Rowena and she carried with her the memory of laughter.

Rowena knew that the old witch lived
in a cottage, somewhere in the woods.
"If I can find the cottage," she thought,
"perhaps I can find where the old woman
has hidden our laughter."

So one morning, she left home and
set out to find the witch's cottage.

But the witch was clever! She looked into her
crystal ball and saw Rowena walking, alone,
in the woods.   "Are you looking for me?"
smiled the old witch.
"Well, you shall find me, my dear.
You shall find me!"

Then she threw back
her head and laughed.

She laughed such a wicked laugh
that the raven flew off her shoulder
in a flurry of black feathers. And
Midnight, her cat, hid under
the table.

Rowena walked and walked.
She scratched herself on thorns;
branches tore her clothing,
but, still, she did not stop.

The sun was high and the day was hot. Before long,
she grew very tired. So, she lay down to rest beneath
a tall pine tree, and soon she was fast asleep.

While she slept, a fairy appeared.
"I have come to warn you," the
fairy said. "The wicked witch
knows you are here. She
will try to trick you,
so you must be very,
very careful. When
she is close enough to
touch, you must catch her.
Then, no matter what happens,
you must not let her go, until she
promises to grant your wish."

When Rowena awakened,
the fairy was gone.
"What a funny dream,"
she thought.

Then, because it was getting late,
she got to her feet and continued on her way.

Soon, a strange little bird cried out to her. "Help me, Rowena! My baby has fallen from its nest. Come, quickly, before the fox finds out, and has it for his dinner!"

Rowena was surprised to hear a talking bird.

Then she remembered the fairy's warning: *The witch knows you are here and she will try to trick you.*

So she said,
"I'm coming, little bird.
But stay close to me,
so I can follow you."

"Wait, little bird," cried Rowena.
But the bird led Rowena deeper and deeper
into the forest. Then Rowena said, "If you go
so quickly, I will not be able to follow.
Stay close to me, so I can see where
you are going."

But again, the bird flew ahead
and Rowena was forced to run after it.

At last, they came to a patch of thorns. "In there," said the bird. "My poor little baby is in there!"

But Rowena was clever, too. "I cannot find an opening in the patch of thorns," she called. "Come here and show me the way."

The bird would not come any closer. It screeched and squawked and scolded. But Rowena would not budge.

At last, the bird came closer. "Hurry!" it scolded. "The fox must have eaten my baby by now."

Rowena moved quickly. Suddenly, she grabbed the bird and held it as tightly as she could.

"Let me go!" screamed the bird. "Let me go!"

But Rowena would not let go. "First you must promise
to grant my wish, old witch!" she cried.

Then the witch knew she had been tricked. She
twisted and turned and tried to escape,
but Rowena held her tightly.

"Let me go.

Let me go."

Suddenly . . . the angry witch
turned herself into a huge dog.
"Let me go," said the dog,
"or I will eat you up."

But Rowena would not let go.

Then . . . the angry witch
turned herself into a terrible monster.
"Let me go," said the monster,
"or I will turn you to stone."

But Rowena would not let go.

Then . . . the witch turned herself into a lion. She turned herself into a giant. She turned herself into a huge rat.

But Rowena would not let go.

At last, the witch knew that she had lost.
"All right," she said. "Name your wish
and be done with it."

"I wish that Pleasantville was a happy place again," said Rowena. "I wish for laughter and I wish for smiles."

The old witch gnashed her teeth, but she had to grant Rowena her wish because she had promised.

"I'm done for,"
    she cried.

She led Rowena into the heart of the forest
and there, in a small clearing,
stood the cottage.

In they went, until they came to a dark staircase that led to the witch's cellar. What was down there?

At the bottom of the stairs, the witch
pointed to a heavy door. Rowena could hear
tiny sounds of laughter coming from behind it.
As she got closer, the sounds got louder and louder.

Hee Hee!

HO HO

Ha! Ha!

WHOOP

ho ho ho

She threw the door open,
and all the smiles and giggles
and grins and laughter came
rushing out with a whoop!

They gathered, like a whirlwind,
spinning faster and faster. Then they
caught up the old witch and carried her up the
stairs, out of the house, and up, up, up in the air.

Away she went,
carried on a whirlwind of laughter.
Higher and higher she flew, until she was
only a tiny speck in the sky.

When Rowena got home, there was a big celebration.
People danced in the streets. The air was filled with
the happy sound of children laughing. Parents smiled,
and friends kissed and made up, and the wicked
old witch was never seen or heard from again.